your tough times bring out
the worst of people but the best of you.

nkh.i

they say never to tell your sadness.
no one cares anyways.
but here I am, writing it all away.
I don't care either.

nkh.i

he said,
"pray, baby. pray."
and so she did,
with her blood and sweat.
she becomes goddess herself.

nkh.i

Life Pro-tips #1

Most of the time they lie when they say they are going to stay.

nkh.i

be kind.
we are all only human after all.

nkh.i

there is no need to rush,
things don't happen on our time.
I know you've heard this before,
but keep on trying.

nkh.i

she was never excellent and never will be.
but all along she has always been herself,
that many did not get to be.

nkh.i

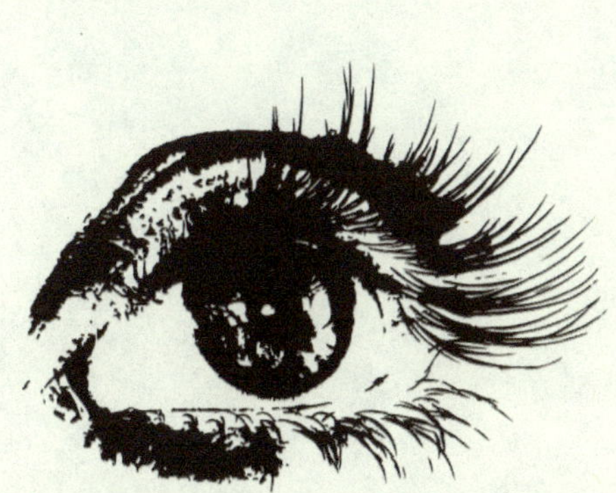

love all with all the love,
but love yourself the most.

nkh.i

just like how you still feel sadness
as if it was yesterday,
even after years, that is how short life is.

nkh.i

in silent whisper,
she screams out her every prayer.
hoping there is someone dear,
to listen and to hear.

nkh.i

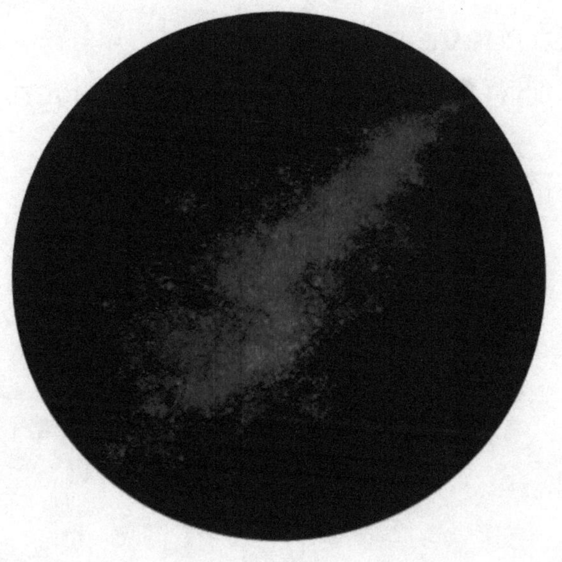

to have money is nice.
to have peace of mind is nicer.
to have both is heavenly.

nkh.i

faith of a child, innocent and kind.
pain of a man, wounding and cruel.
oh, so so fragile.
that is all we are.

nkh.i

it is perfectly okay to be yourself.
look at yourself. awesome af.

nkh.i

breathe, baby. breathe.

nkh.i

the daughter.
the soft and kind one.
always smiling,
hiding her every wounds.
in her own ways,
she tries to ease her pain.
in her own ways,
she tries to bring her happiness.
she is never enough.
she calls her names.
so she stays away,
leaving her with questions, unanswered.

---

nkh.i

in a world so fast,
take time to slow down and unwind.

nkh.i

at the end of the day,
it is you alone with you.
so feed you, first.
love you, first.

nkh.i

pray for the situations to be easier,
but also pray for you to be stronger.

nkh.i

embrace your ups and downs.
be kindest and softest with yourself.
you need you.

nkh.i

the son.
the forever young and wild.
he was his biggest enemy.
he bears the pain of another man
who was supposed to be.
now, a father. he makes sure his sons
have the love he never gets.

nkh.i

I have my coffee unsweetened
because I know I am the sugar.

nkh.i

hehe.

nkh.i

always love like never before.
so when it is gone,
it will always be their lost.
nkh.i

passion needs patience.

nkh.i

sometimes when I'm sad,
I draw a little, doodle a little.
only to feel my inner child smiling.
nkh.i

the daughter.
at her every step
up and down the stairs,
she wished she was good enough
to make her
old lady proud,
almost anything, to make her call her,
"that's my daughter."

nkh.i

abundance, abundance, abundance.
I am blessed.
I am blessed.
I am blessed.
blessing is me.

---

nkh.i

to do list

1. live

nkh.i

often in pain, will I find voices.
voices asking me to be strong.
voices telling me I am not alone.
voices reminding me of who I am.
those voices are me.

---

nkh.i

if you find things funny, laugh.
if you find things sad, cry.
it is okay to show how you feel.
nkh.i

sometimes,
god really sees me as one of
his strongest soldiers.
and I really don't know
how to feel about it.

nkh.i

sad, sad, sad
and nothing else.

nkh.i

to disappear away is nice.
but to be found is nicer.

nkh.i

my mother once said,

"make yourself useful in every situation,
but know when they are just using you."

I didn't understand then, now I know.

nkh.i

they can say anything all they want.

your destiny is in your hands,
in your every thoughts and your feelings.

nkh.i

they say heaven is somewhere far away.

I say, heaven is simply where ticking time doesn't exist.

---

nkh.i

use your energy to create, grow and heal
protect it with your life.

nkh.i

one step at a time.
don't underestimate your little progress.
progress is progress.
nkh.i

overthinking is nice to do sometimes.
you get to think of
the moons and the stars,
how they are shining so bright,
bringing light and smiles on faces.
all,
while you are stuck in a dark quiet room.

nkh.i

it will never be easy
but never invalidate your own feelings.
colors don't change.
a red flag is a red flag.

nkh.i

forgive those who hurt you.
forgive yourself too.

nkh.i

magic. we are all magic.
nobody knows
what is going on on the inside,
but still we make things happen.
magic. we are all magic.

nkh.i

you're not always going to make it on the first try.
but that is what beautiful about life.
every new day is a new chance to begin.
nkh.i

no one is coming to save you.
they don't have to.
they can't.
it's you.
it's you.
it's you who have to do it.

nkh.i

in her melancholy
that she found her light
something that made her feel,
something that lets her live.

nkh.i

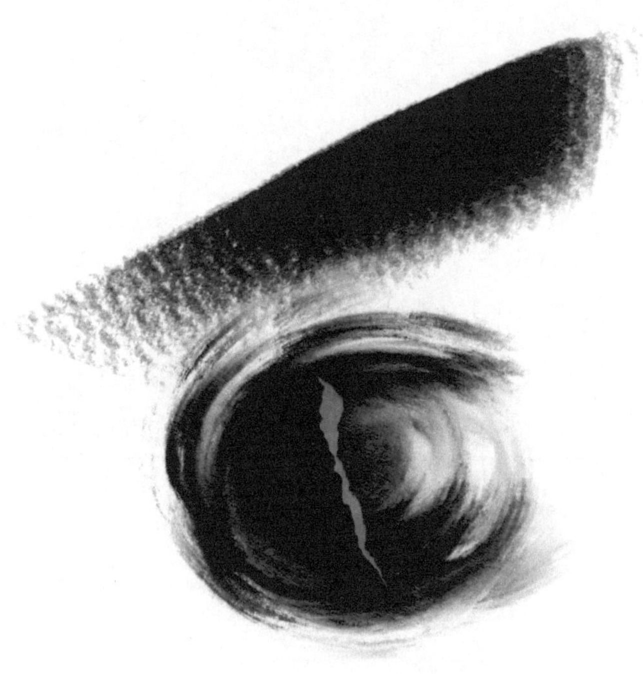

www.ingramcontent.com/pod-product-compliance
Lightning Source LLC
LaVergne TN
LVHW040925150826
845672LV00007B/2213